WS RA C8
IA 9-12

AR
BL 3,6

D0505198

Bungee Hero

by

Julie Bertagna

Illustrated by 700026209458

WORCESTERSHIRE COUNTY
COUNCIL

I	9 4 5
BfS	17 Sep 2004
	£ 4.99

You do not need to read this page -
just get on with the book!

Published in 2004 in Great Britain by
Barrington Stoke Ltd, Sandeman House, Trunk's Close,
55 High Street, Edinburgh EH1 1SR

This edition based on *Bungee Hero*, published by
Barrington Stoke in 2000

Copyright © 2004 Julie Bertagna
Illustrations © Martin Salisbury

The moral right of the author has been asserted in
accordance with the Copyright, Designs
and Patents Act 1988

ISBN 1-84299-209-0

Printed in Great Britain by Bell & Bain Ltd

Meet The Author – Julie Bertagna

What is your favourite animal?
A tiger
What is your favourite boy's name?
Michael
What is your favourite girl's name?
Natalie
What is your favourite food?
Peking duck with Chinese
pancakes
What is your favourite music?
Loud and lots of it!
What is your favourite hobby?
Buying too many CDs

Meet The Illustrator – Martin Salisbury

What is your favourite animal?
Any wild cat
What is your favourite boy's name?
Charles
What is your favourite girl's name?
Stella
What is your favourite food?
Sausages and mash
What is your favourite music?
Patsy Cline
What is your favourite hobby?
Collecting illustrated books

For heroic moments
And to Sandra, for the idea

Contents

Chapter 1

Adam Meets a Grumpy Hero

Adam kicked the ball hard and it shot past the goalie. Yes! It was in! The huge crowd rose to its feet and yelled. Adam held up his arms to them. He was a hero.

"Hurry up and get in the car, Adam."

"Aw, Mum," said Adam with a groan. "Do I have to?"

His dream faded. The crowd in the stands had gone and so had the two football teams. Adam was back in his own garden. He took one last shot at his pretend football, aiming at the living-room window. Then he got in the car.

Mum had been watching him. "You'll have to pay for that smashed window," she told him. Mum might be a pain in the neck about some things but she could take a joke.

"Do we have to go to that stupid old people's home today?" Adam said. "Everyone else goes down to the burger bar after school on a Friday."

"They can do without you for an hour," Mum told him. "Anyway, I only need you to shift a few boxes. It'll do you good. A football hero has to keep fit."

"Not if I'm only a hero in my dreams," Adam said as they drove off to the old people's home. "I can just pretend I'm fit."

Adam's mum was a helper at the old people's home. Sometimes Adam came along to help out.

Mum loved to hear the old people tell
stories about their lives. But they bored
Adam out of his mind. It was worst on
Fridays after school, when he should have
been down at the burger bar, making plans
for the weekend with Micko and Gary.

"Did I tell you old Mrs Carey was once a cancan dancer?" said Mum. "Hard to believe, isn't it?"

She can't have been, thought Adam. She was just a boring old thing, like all the others.

Adam went down to the basement and began taking boxes of tinned food up to the kitchen. It took ages. Mum still wasn't ready when he'd finished.

"It won't kill you to wait a bit longer, Adam," she told him. "I just want to take Mr Haddock out for a bit of fresh air. He's been in bed all week with a horrid cold."

Adam looked at his watch. He was so bored that waiting a bit longer *might* kill him. Micko and Gary would go off without him if he didn't get down to the burger bar soon.

Mum went and fetched Mr Haddock. *Funny name*, Adam thought. *Does he look like a large fish? Is he like an old haddock who tells long, boring tales about his long, boring life swimming round and round in the boring sea?*

But in the end Mr Haddock was just a dull old man in a wheelchair. Adam began to kick his pretend football about in front of the wheelchair as Mum pushed it round the garden.

"Adam!" hissed Mum, as he kicked the ball over the old man's head.

Mr Haddock looked at Adam with angry, cold blue eyes.

"If I was that boy, *I'd* rather pretend to play football than trail along behind an old man in a wheelchair," Mr Haddock said.

The football game in Adam's head melted away. Mum gave him an angry look. Adam walked behind Mum and Mr Haddock for the rest of the walk without saying a word. He didn't want to risk losing his burger money.

"Mr Haddock was in a parachute regiment in the Second World War, Adam," said Mum, as they walked back to the home. "He won a medal for bravery."

"So what?" Adam said, sulking. He looked at his watch again. Micko and Gary would have given up on him by now. The last thing he needed was for this old soldier to start to natter on about the Second World War.

But the old man just looked over the gardens with his angry eyes.

"That's just what I think," Mr Haddock said. "Like the boy says, so what?"

Adam was shocked. He'd thought the old man was too deaf to hear what he had said.

Mum looked really angry now.

"I'm so sorry about Adam, Mr Haddock," she said. "He's longing to be off with his mates. And he's hungry. That's what's making him so rude."

"Ah," said Mr Haddock. He gave Adam another sharp look. "I see."

"Bye," said Adam softly, as Mum pushed the old man up the ramp and in through the door. Mr Haddock didn't even look at him.

Funny, thought Adam, *Mr Haddock really does look a bit like a fish*. He had a long face and a sad mouth and those angry blue eyes. Maybe there was a fish tail under the thick rug that was tucked round the old man. He took another look.

Then Adam got a big shock. The rug lay flat against the leg rest of the wheelchair. The foot rest was empty, too.

Mr Haddock couldn't have been a parachutist in the Second World War.

The old man had no legs.

Chapter 2
Mr Vertigo

"Are you sure Mr Haddock's not just telling a story when he says he was a war hero?" Adam asked on the way home.

Mum shook her head.

"Mr Haddock's mind is OK. And he hasn't always been an old man in a wheelchair. There are some faded photos in his room. One is of a boy about your age, with a

football at his feet. I'm sure it's him. The other is of a young man making a parachute landing. I'm sure that's him, too. He was very good-looking."

Adam couldn't think of the angry old man in the wheelchair as a boy playing football *or* a good-looking, young parachutist.

"How did he lose his legs?" he asked.

"I don't know," said Mum. "You can't really ask, can you?"

Mum stopped the car outside the burger bar. Micko and Gary were sitting by the window where they could stare at passing girls.

"See, they haven't gone without you," said Mum. "There was no need to be rude to Mr Haddock."

"Sorry," said Adam. He gave Mum a sweet smile. "I did lift all those boxes," he told her.

"You did," she smiled, handing him his burger money. "But next time have a little more respect for an old man who risked his life for you."

For me? thought Adam, as he went up for his burger and Coke. *Nothing to do with me. I wasn't even born.*

But, as he waited his turn, Adam began to wonder what it was like being a war hero. What it was like to parachute from a plane and land in enemy country. To face real danger.

"Where were you?" said Micko, when Adam at last joined them. "There's a fair down by the river. Get a move on with that burger and we'll head down there."

Gary grinned. "Mr Vertigo's Big Wheel is gi-normous. The biggest in Europe. You can see it from my bedroom window."

Adam gulped down the last of his burger.

"Great. Let's go!"

****

The fair was next to the river. As it grew dark, the bright lights shone in the water. The river bank was full of people and noise and colour.

By the time Adam and his friends got there, the fair was in full swing. They made for Mr Vertigo's Big Wheel. *It's gi-normous*, thought Adam. His heart thudded in his chest as he looked up at the seats spinning high up into the night sky.

People were coming off Mr Vertigo's Big Wheel, still laughing and yelling. All at once, Adam knew he didn't want to go on it. He was too scared. But if he chickened out, Micko and Gary would annoy him about it for the rest of his life. He *had* to do it.

As he locked the safety bar across his seat, Adam wished he could get off. The seats swayed and jerked as he swung up higher and higher into the dark sky. He was scared stiff.

At the top of Mr Vertigo's Big Wheel, Adam felt awful. He was higher than the huge crane that sat on the bank of the river. He could see to the edges of the city. The river ran for miles.

He was so high he felt sick.

Adam shut his eyes as the wheel started with a jerk. The seats bucked wildly up and down. Then they plunged down, fast and hard. Adam yelled.

The seats tipped forwards. When Adam opened his eyes again he was racing towards the ground. He was going to smash to earth!

At that moment the seats jerked back up as the Big Wheel spun up to the sky once more. For a moment Adam felt better –

until he saw that he would have to do it all again.

And again, and again, until the Big Wheel stopped at last.

When Adam got off the Big Wheel, his heart was still thumping. He had felt sick with fear. But deep inside, he had been thrilled, too.

"I did it!" Adam yelled, as he raced to the dodgems with Micko and Gary. "I really did it!"

All of a sudden he thought of Mr Haddock, not as an angry old man in a wheelchair but as a young parachutist. He saw him dropping out of the sky and crashing to earth.

Had Mr Haddock felt the same strange mix of thrill and fear that Adam had felt as he fell out of the sky on Mr Vertigo's Big Wheel?

Chapter 3
The War Diary

Adam thought about Mr Haddock all week. He didn't know why, but as the week went on he played less and less pretend football. Adam began to see himself as a Second World War parachutist, dropping into enemy country. He had a secret task to do.

"You don't need to come with me to the home today, Adam," Mum told him on

Friday afternoon. "You go off and enjoy yourself."

"Oh," said Adam.

Mum looked at him. "What's the matter?"

"Nothing," said Adam. "It's just that I was planning to take Mr Haddock out for a walk."

"Mr Haddock!" cried Mum. "Why him? You didn't get on with him very well last week."

"What do you mean?" asked Adam.

"Oh come on, Adam," said Mum. "What are you up to?"

"Nothing," Adam told her and added, "It's just that we're doing the Second World

War in school and I want to ask him something."

"Oh, homework," nodded Mum. "Why didn't you say so? Well, make sure you're polite to him this time."

"I'll be an angel," grinned Adam.

****

Mr Haddock wasn't in the mood for a visit from Adam.

"What do you want?" he grumbled, when Adam tapped on his door and asked if he'd like some fresh air. "Has your mother given you extra pocket money to visit me, eh?"

"No," said Adam.

Could this grumpy old man ever have been a brave, young war hero?

Adam was glad to get behind the wheelchair where he could escape Mr Haddock's angry looks. He pushed the old man into the garden. Why had he bothered to come?

"Now, why would a young lad like you want to push a grumpy old man around when you could be off with your friends?" Mr Haddock asked Adam all of a sudden. How did he know what Adam was thinking?

"I – I don't know," said Adam. "I just – I wanted to ask you about the war."

"Ah," said Mr Haddock. "Homework, is it?"

"Yes ... I mean no ... I mean," Adam said with a sigh. What *was* it he wanted to ask? "You see, I was on Mr Vertigo's Big Wheel the other day, at the fair. It was so ..."

Adam stopped. He didn't want to admit to a war hero how scared he had been.

"It was amazing," Adam went on. "And I thought it must be a bit like a parachute jump."

"So you want to know what it's like doing a parachute jump, eh?" barked Mr Haddock. "Well, I've never been on a Big Wheel. But getting ready to jump from a plane as you fly over enemy country is like getting ready to jump into hell. It's no fairground ride, that I can tell you. You don't risk your life on a Big Wheel, do you?"

"No," said Adam.

This old man was awful. Adam turned the wheelchair round and pushed it back to the home. He parked Mr Haddock in front of the TV without saying a word, and went to wait by the car for his mum.

He should never have come. It had been
a waste of time.

****

On Monday morning a parcel arrived in the post for Adam.

"Who's sent you a present?" asked his dad.

"Don't know," said Adam as he tore it open. Inside was a brown leather notebook. PLEASE RETURN TO E. HADDOCK, said a note stuck on the front.

Adam looked inside. The pages were yellow with age and were full of tiny writing. Dust rose from the pages as he flicked through them.

"Adam!" Mum flapped her hand in front of her face. "I'm getting dust in my cornflakes."

Adam stopped at one page and read:

May 17th 1944. 22.20 hours

Just about to leave on my third trip over France.

We have to map out where the enemy troops are in the north.

We shall be in more danger than ever tonight.

So far we've just had a bit of sniper gunfire to dodge. But we'll get the anti-aircraft gunners tonight. A last cuppa, then, we're off.

****

10.00 hours

Back in one piece! Could kill for a bacon butty.

****

Below this, the words were scrawled and hard to read:

Jack's plane didn't make it back. My best buddy. I feel he's going to walk in the door any moment, yelling for his bacon butty. Will he?

****

"Time for school, Adam, and you've had no breakfast," said Mum.

"What's this great book you've got then?" asked Dad. "It must be something pretty good to stop you eating your breakfast."

Adam felt dazed.

"It's from Mr Haddock," he said. "He's sent me his war diary."

Chapter 4
Drop Zone Disaster

Adam put Mr Haddock's war diary in his school bag but it was break-time before he could look at it again. In the playground he flicked over the dusty pages, trying to find the bit he had read at breakfast.

What had happened to Jack, Mr Haddock's best buddy? Did he get back safely? Was his plane shot down? Adam hadn't been able to think of anything else all morning.

Mr Haddock's writing was hard to read, and Adam couldn't remember the date on the page he had found at breakfast. When the bell rang at the end of break, Adam still hadn't found out what had happened to Jack.

It took Adam half of his lunch break to find the right page. Jack's plane *had* been shot down over France by anti-aircraft gunners. He never came back. Mr Haddock lost his best buddy.

Adam showed Micko the war diary and told him all about it.

"One day you're best mates and the next day one of you is dead," said Micko. "How weird."

The two boys looked at each other for a
moment. How awful it must have been.
Adam wasn't sure if he wanted to read any
more of the diary. He liked playing war
games on his computer, but Mr Haddock's

diary wasn't a game. It was real. It hurt him to read it.

Adam took the diary up to his room after dinner that evening. He started to read it from the start.

He read about the hard training Mr Haddock had to have to become a

How awful to lose your best friend

parachutist. He read about his night-time trips flying over France. Once again he read about Jack's death.

It seemed Mr Haddock had no time to take in his friend's death before he was sent off on a new mission. There would be more danger than ever.

****

May 24th 1944

"You don't get to be a war hero because you kill the enemy," our mission leader said tonight. "And being scared doesn't mean that you are a coward. What makes you a hero is that you set others free."

But I don't want to be a hero any more. I thought I did. Both Jack and I did. Now he's dead and tonight I'd give

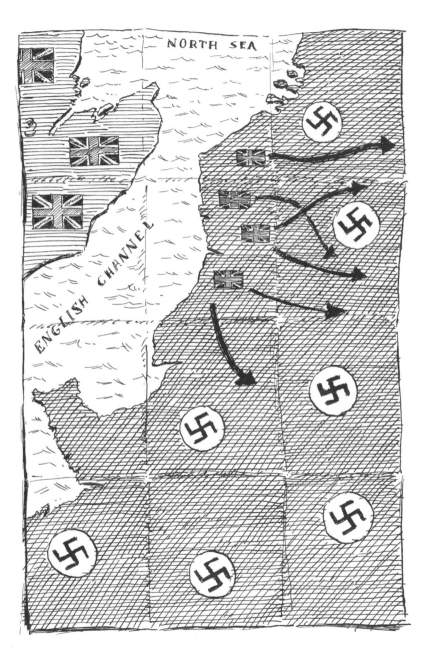

anything to get back to my old life, playing a game of football with my best buddy. Yet the lives of so many people depend on this mission. Hitler's armies are on the move across France and we must help the Resistance forces in their fight against them.

Tonight I must parachute into enemy country. I've only ever done practice jumps before. This will be the real thing. The plane lights will switch off as we reach our drop zone. I will take my place and get ready to jump out of the plane. Below me will be black, empty space. When we spot the signal – the single beam of a torch shining in a field – I must jump. I'll fall into thin air. I can only pray that the enemy is not waiting for me down there and I make a safe landing.

I'm sick with fear. But I must do it. The mission must succeed. I will do it for Jack.

The next page was blank. It seemed to be the end of the diary. Then Adam found one more entry a few pages on.

November 1945

The war is now over. And today I found this old diary again. I could hardly bear to read it. This will be my last entry. I don't know why I'm writing it. Who will ever read this diary but me?

That night of the mission, we flew over the drop zone, but there was no torch signal. We thought that they had forgotten to come. We didn't want to think they had been taken prisoner, or killed. But I had papers to give to the Resistance. I had to make the jump.

I will never forget the moment I fell out of the plane into the icy wind. It was sheer terror! There was a great jolt as my parachute opened. Then there was the most amazing feeling as I floated down.

It was the feeling of being truly alive. "I did it!" I told myself as I crashed to earth.

A moment later the world exploded in my face.

This wasn't the drop zone. It was the wrong field. I had landed on a minefield.

I woke up days later in terrible pain in a strange bed. They told me I'd lost my legs in the blast. I wished I was dead. I had failed. I was no hero.

But they told me I was a hero. The papers I had strapped to my chest were still there when the Resistance found me. They used them to save many lives. All those lives must be worth the loss of one man's legs.

I lost my freedom so that others could be free.

****

Adam shut the diary. He felt odd. But then he had an amazing idea.

It felt like his mission. The mission of his life.

Chapter 5
Mission Bungee

"A parachute jump?" said Micko. "Are you off your head?"

Micko and Gary stared at Adam, amazed.

"How can you do a parachute jump when you were so scared on the Big Wheel?" said Gary. "I saw you."

"I was not!" Adam lied. "And I didn't chicken out, did I?"

"How do you get to do a parachute jump?" asked Micko.

"I haven't a clue," Adam said. "Any ideas?"

Gary looked blank.

Micko gave a shrug.

"Look it up in the Yellow Pages?" said Adam.

****

The first number Adam phoned almost stopped his mission in life before it had even begun.

"Sorry, son. You've got to be over 16 to do a parachute jump," the man on the phone told him.

Adam gave a groan.

"Mission is off," he told the others.

"A mission, is it?" said the voice on the phone. "Does it have to be a parachute jump?"

"Yeah," said Adam.

"Pity," said the man, "because there's always bungee jumping. That's as close as you can get."

"A bungee jump!" yelled Adam. He was so excited he dropped the phone. "That'll do. I'll make it Mission Bungee!"

****

"Your mum will go bananas," said Adam's dad when he heard about Mission Bungee. "Forget it, Adam."

"But it's in a good cause," Adam said.

"It's in a very good cause. I just don't like the idea of it and neither will your mum," said his dad.

Adam's mum didn't go bananas. She just said no.

Adam was about to storm up to his room when he had a good idea. He picked up Mr Haddock's war diary.

"Listen to this," he said.

He read the bit about Jack and the entry written the night before Mr Haddock's parachute jump. Then he read the last entry of all.

"Fifty years in a wheelchair," said Dad at last. "And there must be so many other young men like Mr Haddock who spent the rest of their lives in hospitals and homes."

"It's very sad," said Mum. "But I don't see why Adam should risk his life in a bungee jump."

"I'm not risking my life," Adam said. "I'll have a safety harness and helmet. The experts will be there to see I'm OK."

"But why?" Mum wanted to know.

"I want to do this jump to get sponsor money for an electric wheelchair. Mr Haddock can't wheel himself about any more. It'll give him more freedom. He deserves that."

Adam remembered the words in Mr Haddock's diary. How the thrill and terror of the parachute jump was the feeling of being truly alive.

"I really want to do it," Adam told his parents.

"All right," said Mum at last. "If you can prove to me it's safe, you can do it. But don't come crying to me if you break your neck!"

****

"Ready?" asked the bungee instructor.

Adam was in a panic. He would never be ready. This was a mad idea – a very bad, mad idea. He no longer cared if he chickened out and made a fool of himself in front of Mum and Dad, Micko and Gary, the newspaper reporters, and all the kids and teachers from school. He was too scared to care. He just could not do it.

Mission Bungee had become famous. "Do it somewhere odd," the instructor had said, "then you'll get a big crowd. The more people you get, the more money you'll raise." So Adam chose the huge crane down by the river, the one he had seen from the top of the Big Wheel that night at the fair. The bungee instructors had checked it out and said it was perfect.

Now he was standing on top of the crane in front of a huge crowd, getting ready to do a bungee jump.

Adam looked across at the Big Wheel on the other side of the river. Mr Haddock was right. A ride on that was a joke compared to this. Yet even a bungee jump couldn't be as scary as a parachute jump. One that landed you in enemy country, right on top of an exploding mine.

You didn't even hit the ground in a bungee jump. You just landed upside down in mid-air at the end of an elastic safety rope.

I'll die of fear, thought Adam.

Then he saw Mr Haddock in his wheelchair, beside Mum and Dad. When he had told Mr Haddock about the bungee jump and why he was doing it, the old man's angry eyes had filled with tears. Then they'd had a long talk.

Now, as Adam looked down, the old man saluted him.

Adam got ready to jump. He could chicken out in front of everyone else but he could not let Mr Haddock down.

What was it Mr Haddock's mission leader had said in the war diary? Being scared doesn't make you a coward. But giving freedom to someone else makes you a hero.

Adam shut his eyes. He counted to three.

Then he let himself fall.

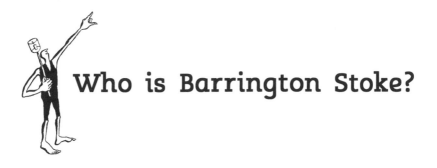

Who is Barrington Stoke?

Barrington Stoke went from place to place with his lamp in his hand. Everywhere he went, he told stories to children. Some were happy, some were sad, some were funny and some were scary.

The children always wanted more. When it got dark, they had to go home to bed. They went to look for Barrington Stoke the next day, but he had gone.

The children never forgot the stories. They told them to each other and to their children and their grandchildren. You see, good stories are magic and they can live for ever.

If you loved this story, why don't you read ...

Hostage

by Malorie Blackman

Can you imagine how frightened you would be if you were kidnapped? Angela is held to ransom and needs all her skill and bravery to survive.

4u2read.ok!

You can order this book directly from our website
www.barringtonstoke.co.uk

If you loved this story, why don't you read ...

Resistance

by Ann Jungman

Do you ever disagree with your parents? Jan is ashamed when his Dutch father sides with the Germans during the Second World War. Only Elli is his friend. Can Jan find a way to help the Resistance?

You can order this book directly from our website
www.barringtonstoke.co.uk

If you loved this story, why don't you read ...

The House with No Name

by Pippa Goodhart

Can secrets live on after death? Jamie moves into a house that has been empty for thirty-five years. He discovers a tragic secret from the past. Find out what Jamie comes across in the House with No Name.

4u2read.ok!

You can order this book directly from our website
www.barringtonstoke.co.uk

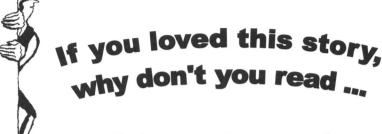

If you loved this story, why don't you read ...

Tod in Biker City

by Anthony Masters

Could you survive in a world that had become a total desert? Tod's father finds a source of water but his discovery puts the whole family in great danger. It's up to Tod to save them!

4u2read.ok!

You can order this book directly from our website
www.barringtonstoke.co.uk

If you loved this story, why don't you read ...

Tod and the Sand Pirates

by Anthony Masters

Have you ever had to fight for your life? The whole world is suffering from a lack of water. There is a huge fuel shortage too. Tod and Billy are looking for a new water supply, when pirates take them prisoner. How will they escape?

4u2read.ok!

You can order this book directly from our website
www.barringtonstoke.co.uk

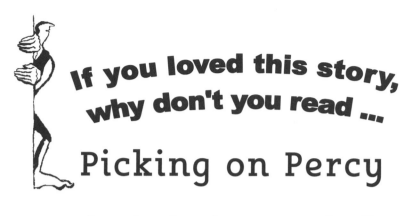

If you loved this story,
why don't you read ...

Picking on Percy

by Catherine MacPhail

Has anyone ever picked on you?
Shawn is making Percy's life a misery.
But he is in for a shock when he
discovers to his horror that he is living
Percy's life!

4u2read.ok!

You can order this book directly from our website
www.barringtonstoke.co.uk